To Alex
with Love
from Randi &
Dr. Savos

For Aunt Dee and Uncle Paul
and their delightful tribe
J. H.

To Amelia,
with thanks
I. B.

Text copyright © 2002 by Judy Hindley
Illustrations copyright © 2002 by Ivan Bates

First U.S. edition 2002

Library of Congress Cataloging-in-Publication Data

Hindley, Judy.
Do like a duck does / Judy Hindley ;
illustrated by Ivan Bates. —1st U.S. ed.
p.   cm.
Summary: By challenging a hairy stranger to imitate the
behavior of herself and her ducklings, a mother duck proves
that he is a fox and not a duck.
ISBN 0-7636-1668-0
[1. Ducks—Fiction. 2. Foxes—Fiction. 3. Stories in rhyme.]
I. Bates, Ivan, ill. II. Title.
PZ8.3.H5555 Do 2002
[E]—dc21   2001025681

10 9 8 7 6 5 4 3 2 1

Printed in Hong Kong

This book was typeset in Stempel Schneidler and Metropolis.
The illustrations were done in watercolor.

Candlewick Press
2067 Massachusetts Avenue
Cambridge, Massachusetts 02140

visit us at www.candlewick.com

Do Like a Duck Does!

Judy Hindley

illustrated by

Ivan Bates

CANDLEWICK PRESS
CAMBRIDGE, MASSACHUSETTS

Five little ducklings,
following their
mother;

whatever
any duck does,
so does every other.

So they waddle and they hop
and they scuttle and they stop —

Flop! Flop! Flop! Flop! Flop!

All together.

"Quack!" says Mama Duck.

"That's the way to be!

Do like a duck does!

Do like me!"

There go the ducklings, all in a line.
But who's creep-creeping close, following behind?

"Wait!" says Mama, "You don't belong with us —
Stop!" says Mama. "Do you think you're a duck?"

"But of course!" says the stranger, with a waddle and a strut. "That's just what I am — a big, brown duck."

Well, he has no feathers
and he has no beak.
He has four claws
on his hairy-scary feet.
He has two ears
that stick up a mile,
and a wicked
foxy nose and
a wicked
foxy smile.

So Mama says, "Well, then, do like us.
Head up, tail up, toes pointing out.
Stretch your little wings, dear,
straighten up your back.
Do like a duck does —

**Quack!
Quack!
Quack!"**

Then Mama leads
them off together —

Hup! Hup! Hup!

Five little ducklings and a big brown duck —
a hairy-scary stranger — a very silly duck!

"Look!" says Mama.
"What a lovely patch of muck!
Jump in the puddle, dear.
Show you're a duck!
Lots of bugs and beetles
swimming in the scum.
Open up your beak, dear.

Yum!
Yum!
Yum!"

Now the very hairy stranger
has some notions of his own,
and he's looking
at the ducklings
when he says,

**"Yum,
yum!"**

And he's creeping
ever closer . . . and
he's very,
very
near . . .

But Mama turns and catches him
and says, "Look here!
You don't like bugs.
You don't like muck.
You can't say quack. . . .
Are you *sure*
you're a duck?"

"Yes, I am!"
says the stranger.
"It's really, really true!

I can waddle.
I can scuttle.
I can strut a little, too.

I'm a duck!
I'm a duck!
I'm a duck like you!"

So Mama says,
"Show it! Prove you're a duck.
Do like a duck does! Do like us!"
Then they zip through the thistles and . . .

. . . they slip into the river. **Plop! Plop! Plop!**

Plop! Plop! All together.

Down go the ducklings, all tails up! And down goes

the stranger. **Glup! Glup! Glup!**

So where are all the ducklings now?
Here they all come.

Pop!

Pop! Pop! Pop! Pop! Every one.

But where's the
very hairy-scary stranger?

Gone home.

"Well," says Mama.
"What a bit of luck.

But I really always knew . . .

that was no duck!"